My Wealthy Grandfather

Winston Philpott

Best Wishes

Winston Philpott

Outskirts Press, Inc.
Denver, Colorado

My Wealthy Grandfather
All Rights Reserved
Copyright © 2006 Winston Philpott

Outskirts Press
http://www.outskirtspress.com

ISBN-10: 1-59800-364-X
ISBN-13: 978-1-59800-364-2

My Wealthy Grandfather
Would never give up.
Never, never, never.
He would find work
and make money. He
always said there is
one more shot left in
the locker, and while
there is a shot left in
the locker, I will never,
never, never, give up.

Chapter 1

Bill was outside working in the strawberry patch. It was the place he spent most of his spare time when he had a couple days off. Because he worked the weekend, he had Monday and Tuesday off. He sure enjoyed working at the strawberries, as well as eating them and freezing them for the winter. He also enjoyed the other things he grew.

He heard Sadie call him from the back door and went to see what she wanted, thinking maybe she needed something from the store. She told him that he had a call from a lawyer in St. John's. It was the lawyer that his grandfather went to see the last time he was home to Newfoundland, so it was best for him to call him as soon as he could.

He said, "Sadie, I wonder what that is all about? I hope Grandfather has not run up bills and now that he has passed on they want me to pay them because I am the only one left in the family."

It sort of worried Bill, as he was not making that much money working with the town council as a heavy equipment operator.

"Well Sadie, I'd better call them and find out. If it is, we will do the best we can to pay up. I know he bought that truck. Maybe it is not paid for."

Bill made the call to the lawyer's office. The lady at the desk answered. Bill told her that the lawyer asked him to call. "Oh yes. I know about it. Could you come in? The lawyer wants to see you."

"I am free tomorrow only, if I can come and see him then. If not, I have to wait for another week."

The lady said, "How about two tomorrow?"
Bill said that would be fine. "Hope there are no outstanding bills there for me to pay," Bill said to the lady. She told him she didn't think he had to worry about that. "Can't figure out what this is all about. Anyway, whatever it is, we will just have to wait until tomorrow." Then he went back to the garden and the strawberry patch.

At dinner they talked about it. Bill said it couldn't be bills from anything because Grandfather had his mail come to them when he was there and he never saw any bills that came. It was all forwarded on to him, so they just forgot about it.

After supper they put a few things in their bags to get ready for the trip to town. They had a few things to take in to Jessie, his cousin's wife. She was part of the family and was real close to both Sadie and him. She was closer to Sadie than if she were a sister. They visited each other quite often, and she would come and stay two or three days. They would do the same when he could get the time off.

Early the next morning they were off to town, wanting to visit Jessie before going to the lawyer's office, which they did. They got there just in time for morning coffee around ten.

Bill told Jessie why he was in town and about the lawyer calling him and wanting to see him. He also said it was the same lawyer his grandfather went to see when he was here on his last trip home to Newfoundland.

Jessie told Bill that Grandfather always went to that law office when he came in to see her, because she took him there.

Sadie asked Jessie if she would come along with them, because if they had to wait long it would help them to pass the time away and give them someone to talk with. "Okay," Jessie said. "If not, I will be here all day alone. I will get ready now and as soon as we have dinner, we can go. By the time we get there it will be close to two and you won't have too long to wait."

They got to the lawyer's office a little before two and the lady at the desk told them to sit and she would see how long before the lawyer could see them. When she came back, she told them it would be about ten minutes. Bill thanked her and tried to relax, but it wasn't easy. He was just as tense as the two women with him, but he tried not to show it.

The lady at the desk answered the phone. Then she looked at them and told them to come on in, leading the way and offering them chairs while Jessie waited in the waiting room.

Chapter 2

The lawyer came right to the point. "Mr. Jackson, how much did you know about your grandfather?" said Joe Sims.

Bill said, "Not very much. He went away to the USA before I was born. I never saw him until these last two years when he looked us up. I only saw snapshots of him that Mother had. He kept in touch with Mother and would always send her a good Christmas gift of money. He never came down to any funerals. He said that it took too long to get there, ut he always sent the money to pay all the expenses. He always said there was no way he could make it on time, then when Grandmother passed away, he said he wanted to come to Newfoundland and look me up. I am glad that he did. He was a wonderful man. We loved him, and Jessie thought a lot of him as well."

The lawyer asked, "Who is Jessie?"

"Well, Jessie is my cousin's wife. He was killed in

an auto crash and she is here with us today sitting outside."

"Do you have any idea what we want you for today?" the lawyer asked. "Did your grandfather ever tell you what he did for a living in the USA?"

Bill told the lawyer that his grandfather was a carpenter and his mother told him that he was one of the best, and did well working in the States. That was about all he knew. "Grandfather was a very old man when he did visit, and he never talked about anything back in the States. He only wanted to enjoy Newfoundland and trout fishing, when he was able to go. He bought me a good secondhand truck so I could take him fishing whenever I had the time. We never had to take the car from Sadie, as Sadie was involved in many things around the church and needed the car. Grandfather was sure good to us."

"Well," the lawyer said, "you are in for a big surprise. Your grandfather was a multimillionaire. He owned half of New York and now it is all yours. He had it fixed so that as soon as he passed on, your name was next to take over and he never wanted you to know until he was gone. He said he watched you and knew that you were making a living working for the town where you lived, and you were a good worker, and that you could manage things well when he was gone."

Bill turned white and his wife asked him if he was okay. "Yes," he said. "It is quite a shock though. I never thought that he was so rich and he out-lived most of his family where I am the only one left. Jessie is not a blood relation, but she will have her share as well."

"Now, Mr. Jackson, you will have to make a trip to New York as soon as you can to look after your affairs there. You will have to first go to the lawyer's office. They will fill you in on everything. As soon as you can make the trip, phone and let me know and I will pick up the tickets for you."

Bill said, "I will let you know tomorrow after I talk to the town where I work. I just can't walk out on them without letting them know." Then they shook hands and Bill left.

Sadie said, "Maybe Jessie could come along with us, if that is okay with you, Bill?"

"It's okay with me, because Jessie has a share in this as well as I do." Turning to Jessie, Bill told her that she would get a quarter share of everything, so she'd better come along. Jessie told Bill she would talk to them tonight on the phone and let them know for sure if she would go. This took her by so much surprise that it would take a while for it to all sink in.

They dropped off Jessie and drove on home. Not hardly a word was spoken. Bill was trying to come to grips with everything, wondering if it was just a dream. He almost had to punch himself to see if he was still asleep.

After arriving home, it was too late to talk to the town, so the best thing for him to do was go to work tomorrow and then he could tell them, and that is what he did.

Getting to work the next morning, he went right up to the office and told them he wanted time off as he had to go to New York on business about his grandfather's estate. They told him that would be fine as it was the slack time of the year and he could have whatever time he wanted. He left at noon because he had to contact the lawyer's office to make plans for the trip.

At one-thirty he called the lawyers and told them he was ready to go whenever they could arrange it, and to buy tickets for three people. Jessie had phoned Sadie that morning and said she would go. The lawyer told him he would get back to him later that evening, but Bill would have to come to see him before he left because the lawyer had money for him to cover traveling expenses. "Okay," Bill said, "as soon as I hear from you, I will come into town."

The lawyer phoned late that evening and told Bill that he had a flight out in two days for the three of them. Bill should come in tomorrow and pick up the tickets and the money. Then he was on his own to make the next moves. The lawyer told Bill that if he needed him at any time to call, he knew the number.

Bill left early the next morning by himself for St. John's. He saw the lady at the desk and signed for the tickets and five hundred dollars. He didn't stop anywhere else and went home to get ready for the trip to New York. He would leave the car at Jessie's and get a cab to take them all to the airport to catch the flight.

The next morning everything went as planned and before they knew it, they were on the plane for New York.

Chapter 3

Upon arriving in New York they went and got a cab. He didn't know his way around. He gave the cab driver the address to his grandfather's home. In about ten minutes they were there. The lawyer told him to check with the caretaker next door and he would give him the keys. "But you will have to show him who you are by giving him a letter from me or he will not give you the keys."

Bill looked at the home. It was a large home, big enough to be a hotel. Then he went next door and knocked. That house was not so small either. In a short time this older man came to the door. Bill told him who he was. The man looked at him for a minute and then at the cab with the two ladies on board. Then he said, "What have you got to prove who you are?"

Bill said, "I have a letter here from the lawyer back in St. John's, Newfoundland." He then passed it to him.

"So, you are Joe's grandson. Well if you are half as

good as Joe, you are a good man. He was a wonderful man, one of the best. You can tell the cab to go. I will get you the keys to your grandfather's home."

Bill went and paid for the cab, and brought their bags to the front door of his grandfather's home. By that time the caretaker was there. He opened the door and said, "Here it is. It is all yours, a home in New York." The caretaker told them there was very little food there, so if they wanted extra food, there was a food market just five minutes away. He would take them there. As he was leaving, Bill followed him and thanked him. He then told him he wanted to have a talk with him after he had lunch. The caretaker said that he would come back in about an hour. That would give them time for lunch.

There was plenty of most everything in the house. There were some things in the freezer, so they had no trouble making lunch.

It was almost ten at night before the caretaker came over. He made a light tap on the door and came in saying he was sorry, but he had gone to lie down and fallen asleep. He just woke up. Bill said, "That is fine. There is plenty of time. Maybe I should have waited until tomorrow instead of getting you out this late."

"It is okay with me, as I am all alone and have spent many hours here with your grandfather. After your grandmother passed on he felt very lonely and the thing he talked about most was the wonderful time he would spend in Newfoundland with you people. He sure looked forward to it. The last time he made the trip it took everything out of him, but he said he just had to go to see you once more. He told me all about what he was going to do by passing everything over to you and didn't want you to know until he was gone.

"I just can't tell you any more. You will get it all

9

from the lawyer tomorrow." With that he changed the conversation by asking about Newfoundland and telling them that his father came from Newfoundland. It was at his father's that Joe stayed when he came up here until he got a place of his own. He said his family had always been in touch with Joe, right up until he passed on. The caretaker said he would go with them on the bus to the lawyer's office and they could find their own way back.

"Fine," Bill said. "What time will we go? Ten will be okay with me, if that is okay with you?"

"Good Scot," the caretaker said, "from now on just call me Scot. Okay?"

At ten o'clock the next morning they were off. It was a lot different from where they lived and took a lot of getting used to.

Going into this big building, they looked up on the top and it said, "THE SIMS BUILDING." "This is where the lawyer's office is," Scot said, "in your building. See you when you get back," and he was gone.

Chapter 4

Joe left Newfoundland when he was a young man. That summer the fishing failed and not very many people had any money, so carpenter work was very scarce. Joe came home one day and asked Myrtle if she would go to the United States if he went. He said, "We can't stay here and land up on the rocks or not have enough money to go anywhere."

"It's okay with me," she said. "We can never give up. We just have to go where we will make it. I will never give up, never, never."

"Well, I am going to send a wire message to my friend and ask him if we could stay with him if we came up until we get work and a place of our own to live in."

Joe was off to the post office (the telegraph office was then at the post office) the next day. He got an answer back telling him to come on as soon as he could. There was plenty of work up there for someone like him.

There were not so many boats sailing to the United States at that time, but there was a boat leaving for New York in a week. It was first going to Sidney then to New York. They packed whatever they could handle and got on the boat when it left. The trip was long and rough. Plenty of people were seasick, but because he was on the sea so much fishing, he never got sick and he could help Myrtle, as she was sure sick.

After a while they did get to New York and picked up their bags. They caught a taxi and gave the driver the address to his friend's house. A half hour later they were there. They went to the door and they all met them. They even came out and helped them bring in their bags. They were so glad to see them. His friend had been in New York about fifteen years now, had his own home and was working all the time.

They had a good meal and then a good chat about Newfoundland and what it was like back there. It was tough going trying to make a living. Sam said, "I am glad I came up here, but I still love Newfoundland."

Sam told Joe he was going to work tomorrow morning and if he wanted to, he could come with him and check out the place where he worked. They were doing a lot of building and maybe Joe could get a job there.

In the morning Joe was up and away with Sam. He went to check with the man in charge and told him he just came from Newfoundland and was looking for a job as a carpenter. "I have brought some tools, but may have to buy more, as they were too heavy to bring them all."

The manager told him to come with him. He had to go and see the foreman before he could say anything. The foreman said, "Yes, we need half a dozen right now. Can you come tomorrow morning?"

"I'll be here," Joe said. He then caught a cab and went back to where he was staying. He had dinner and went out for a walk to check things out and find his way around.

Joe was only working for a short while when the manager came to him and said the foreman was being transferred to another job. "Would you take his place? I can see you know what you are doing when it comes to carpenter work."

"Well," Joe said, "If you think I can do it, I will. I may need you to guide me sometimes."

"Fine," the manager said, "you can take over tomorrow."

The manager told him that he could have a pickup if he needed it. "Well, I can't even drive yet. I will have to learn first. Then we will see."

Joe was making things move so well that they kept adding more jobs on and before he could think about it, they had him in charge of the whole thing with many foremen under him. After learning to drive, he got the pickup because some of the jobs were miles apart.

Chapter 5

Bill walked inside and walked up a long hall until he saw the lawyer's office. He tapped on the door and went in. He told the man on the desk who he was and that he was there to see the lawyer and wanted to make an appointment. The gentleman said to wait a minute and maybe the lawyer could see him now. "If you can wait, he will see you within minutes," he told him.

"Good, I can wait."

In a short while the lawyer called him in. He told Bill about his grandfather and what he had told them to do. He told Bill that everything now belonged to him. "Your grandfather left everything for us to do until you came up and told us what you wanted to do. In fact, you now own this building and many, many more, and they are all filled and paying well."

Bill stopped and then he said, "It is best to leave everything as is and you people can carry on and look after everything. You can collect your fee and put the remainder in the bank."

"The bank account is now in your name. I will take you to the bank and have things fixed so you can use the money when you want. Later when we have more time, I will take you around and show you what you own.

"There are five hotels plus homes all around the city. The home the caretaker lives in also belongs to you, only your grandfather had it put in his will to let the caretaker stay there rent free as long as he lives, if that is okay with you."

"It sure is," Bill said. "He is a fine man and we need him around."

"He is the son of the friend where your grandfather stayed when he came up here, and he said he was trying to pay back what the caretaker's father did for him."

"There is so much that has happened in these last few days. I will have to go home and have a rest. Then I can digest some more."

The lawyer said, "In a couple of days' time, give me a ring and we can take a run around. Then you will have a better idea about everything you own.

"There are a few things, like paperwork to get fixed up, but that can wait for a while. It will, however, have to be done before you go back to Newfoundland." Bill knew now he was talking to a good lawyer and if he wasn't, his grandfather would never have used him. He could go home and sleep without a worry. Then after a couple of days, he would carry on where his grandfather left off.

After a good night's sleep, Bill asked Sam, the caretaker, if he would mind taking them to a good place to do some shopping. "I know that you know your way around much better than I do." Sam said he would be glad to do that, so after lunch Sam took them in his car and brought them to the largest shopping center they had ever seen. They bought all the things they needed and more besides.

Bill paid Sam extra money for taking them to the store. Sam said, "There is no need. I am getting paid now."

Bill told Sam, "You are getting paid to be a caretaker and not for taking us around, so take the money and use it."

It was hard for Bill to get used to the fact that he was wealthy and owned the home in New York and had a caretaker at his service. It would take a while for him to learn the ropes.

Sadie said, "You have us at your side to help." Jessie was also there and said she would help with anything she could. Bill told her that part of everything belonged to her as well as him.

Sadie said she was feeling a little sick, but she would be okay after a rest. Jessie said to take a good rest as maybe the strain was getting to her. So Sadie went to bed. Bill went out to look around the place. Jessie got a book and spent a few hours reading.

By the time Bill returned, Sadie was up and about feeling much better. They then had supper and sat and watched TV. They got the local news. Bill called the caretaker and asked him if would he like to come and have a coffee with him because he knew he spent plenty of time with his grandfather and now he missed him.

After a good chat, Sam went home and they all went to bed for the night.

Chapter 6

Joe was making so much money for the firm that he was put as top man next to the owner. There he learned the tricks of the trade, buying and selling real estate. He was in contact with the lawyers and got to know them all, as well as all the office staff. He kept things at the office in order so the owner never had to do anything but check in once in a while.

One morning when Joe came in, the owner of the firm called him in. "Joe," he said, "you are doing so good you could run this firm if I wasn't around."

"Well," Joe said, "it's good to have someone check on me sometimes though."

"Well Joe, I have been thinking about retiring and selling out this firm. And I sure would like for you to have it."

Joe said, "I could never come up with the money."

"Joe, if you really want it, I can arrange it for you and within a few years you can own the firm."

"Well if you would do that, I will go through with it and take it over whenever you are ready."

"As of today, you will have the office and the building the office is in, as well as whatever jobs are half finished. If you say yes, I will contact my lawyer today and get the needed papers ready. Come in to the office tomorrow and we will get things passed over to you. I will come in anytime you want me for a while until you figure you can make it alone."

So Joe went on from that and things went so well that in two years he had everything paid for and was making money building homes and buildings. He was also buying older buildings and repairing them, and renting them or selling them whenever he got the right price.

After taking over the firm, one of the employees was retiring, as they were sixty-five, so Myrtle went to work at the office in her place.

Now Joe had a lot of real estate around New York. He bought a large home with extra land so he could block it up and build homes on it. He built a home next to his and asked his friend if he would like to move there and be a caretaker for his home. If he did, it was rent-free and his family would never have to pay rent. So his friend moved into the new home, looked after Joe's place and the lawns, and so on. After his friend was too old to do it, Joe passed it over to his friend's son.

Years passed by fast and Joe became very rich and had some top men looking after things for him so he could leave and do a little traveling. He was getting older and wanted to go back to Newfoundland for a trip and look up some of his kin if there was any left. Two daughters and their husbands had passed on, and he knew that Annie and Norman had one son, his grandchild, named Billie. His other daughter and her husband had passed on as well, and their only son got killed in an auto crash. So if he could do it, he had to find his grandson.

Seeing the lawyer, he told him to watch things for him, as he was taking a trip back to Newfoundland. He would contact him when he got there.

Now it was a lot different from when he came up. You could only make the trip then by boat. It took days. Now you got on a plane and a few hours later, you were there.

He got to St. John's and went to a hotel. After having a meal, he went to bed. It was getting late and he was now an old man and couldn't take it without plenty of rest.

The next morning he checked the phone book for Jacksons. Sure enough, he saw the name "William Jackson." That must be him, he thought, but we always called him Billie. It was early in the morning so he thought he would wait an hour or so, because he might have gone to work and his wife might not be up.

Around ten he called the number and asked for Billie. The lady who answered said he was at work. Then he asked her if Billie was Annie and Norman's son.

"Yes," she said.

"I am coming to see you tonight after he gets off work. I am his grandfather from the States who he has never seen and I've never seen him. I hope this is okay with you."

"Yes," she said, "I have heard him say he would like see his grandfather before he died, because he knew he was getting old and he could never spare the money to go to the States."

Chapter 7

When Bill came home from work, Sadie said, "Who do you think I had a phone call from today?" Bill guessed a few, but never dreamed who it could be. She said, "Your grandfather is in St. John's and is coming out this evening to see you." Before she had told him all about it, there was a knock on the door. Bill went to answer it and he put his arms around his grandfather. He gave him a big hug and shed tears of joy to see him, and likewise did his grandfather.

Grandfather said, "I have a cab hired so I cannot stay too long."

Bill said, "You are not leaving here again this night, so send the cab back to town."

"Well," Joe said, "my bags are all at the hotel."

"That is okay. I will ask for a day off tomorrow and we can go in and get them. If that is what you want to do?"

"It is okay with me," Grandfather said. "Billie, I am

only staying for a week this time. If I live, I will be back again later. I want to go to St. John's to talk to a lawyer. I have a few things to straighten out here in Newfoundland while I am here. As I am getting older, I have to do these things before I pass on. That could happen any day, though I feel good for my age and have good health as of now."

Bill said, "I will go in to work tomorrow morning and talk to the counsel foreman and ask if it would be possible for me to have a week's holiday. I have three weeks owed to me. If so, we can go in tomorrow and pick up your bags and go to see if you can talk to a lawyer the same day."

Grandfather Joe said, "That would be wonderful. It will save me a lot of worry."

Bill never thought any more about it. He just thought maybe it was something from way back when his grandfather lived there and he wanted to get it off his hands. He never thought that he had arranged with his lawyer back in the States to get a lawyer here in Newfoundland to help to pass everything he had over to Bill, but he wanted to meet Bill first and he was quite satisfied now. He had no one else left but Bill, and he did like him. He seemed to be a fine fellow.

Bill got a week off and spent time with Joe. It was just he and his grandfather. Grandfather asked about Jessie, his other grandchild's wife. Bill said, "If you want, we can go in and you can meet her."

"Okay," Grandfather said, "that would be wonderful."

Before they knew it, they were driving in Jessie's driveway. She didn't know they were coming. Bill tapped on the door, opened it and went in. "Jessie, I am surprising you today. This is Grandfather I have here with me. He wanted to see you, as he never met you or his grandson before he got killed in the car crash."

They only stayed for a short while and they were off, as Joe had a lot of work to do before going back. On the way out, Joe said to Jessie, "Sure glad to have met you. Bill and Sadie will make sure you are taken care of." She was wondering what he meant by that.

They went to the hotel first and picked up Joe's bags. Then they went to a lawyer's office. It was one that Bill recommend and had business with himself. Bill waited outside in the waiting room. His grandfather took almost an hour in the law office. When he came out, he looked happy.

"Bill, if you haven't anything to do, I am ready to go back home."

Arriving home, Sadie had a jigs dinner cooked. Grandfather loved it, because the most he ate now was hotel food.

While they were eating supper, Bill asked him if he would like to go fishing tomorrow, because he was off on his holidays and meant to do a little fishing. Grandfather said it was just what he needed now to bust him up a little before he went back. He would not make many more trips back there because he was getting too old to travel. It just depended on his health.

Chapter 8

Joe packed his bags and was ready to catch the plane back to the States that evening. Bill said he would take him to the plane and wait for him to get onboard. Sadie said she would make a few sandwiches for him in case he got hungry. Bill told Sadie to come along and they would stop by Jessie's to say goodbye before going to the airport.

Joe made the flight back without any trouble and his driver was waiting for him, because he had phoned and told him what time he would arrive. He told his driver to take him to his hotel, the hotel he most always stayed at. Then he sent the driver home.

He had a lunch and went to his room. He had a standing room so that at any time he came it was ready, as he owned the hotel anyway. He had a shower and went to bed, as he had a long day ahead.

The next day after breakfast he called his driver, as now he was getting too old to do a lot of driving, but he never had to anyway.

When his driver arrived, he told him to take him to the Simms Building to the law office, and told the driver to wait.

He checked with the office to see if he could see the lawyer or not. The lady on the desk checked with the lawyer. He had someone in the office, but he would see him shortly if he had time to wait. Joe said he would wait.

He went out and told the driver that it would take him maybe an hour or more, and if he wanted to go somewhere, he could. He told Joe that he would go and get a coffee. "Fine," said Joe.

The lawyer called him in and said, "Sorry I was so busy."

"Fine with me," Joe said. "I can wait." Anyway, Joe came right to the point. He told the lawyer to draw up the papers to transfer everything over to his grandson back in Newfoundland. It all should be put in the name of Bill Jackson or William Jackson, with Joe's name second until he passed on. When he did, this lawyer was to contact the lawyer in St. John's at the address he gave him, and advise Bill to come up, take over, and decide what he wanted to do with everything.

"If you can come back tomorrow afternoon, I will have everything ready for you to sign." Joe said to put a note in the papers that Bill was to share what he thought was right with Jessie. She was his other nephew's wife. "Fine," the lawyer said

Joe then told his driver to take him to the office where they kept everything running. The staff said they were glad to see him back and hoped that he had a fine trip. He said that he did. He told them that once he was gone, they would have a new owner, his nephew, but that was to stay within the firm until it came to pass.

Then after the meeting with the office staff, he got the driver to take him back to his home to see the caretaker, and also tell him about it just in case he should pop off. They would know what to expect when he arrived home. Sam was outside his own home doing something on the lawn. He shouted to him and told him to come over and have a coffee with him. He also told the driver to come in with him as well and they would enjoy a coffee and a chat. Although he was a multimillionaire, he would always take time when he could and have coffee with Sam and his driver.

He told them what he had done, all about his nephew, and what would happen once he had passed on. His nephew would take over, but they would be looked after. That was in the papers that he would sign tomorrow.

After a good hour of chatting and drinking coffee, he told the driver to take him to his hotel. He never spent much time at home anymore because everything was done for him at the hotel. After Myrtle, his wife, had passed on, it was too lonely staying there alone.

It had been another long day and he was getting tired. He got a shower and went to bed. He was up early and feeling wonderful. He had a good breakfast and was reading the morning paper when the phone rang. When he answered it, he heard the lawyer wanting some more information. He also told him that he could come in whenever he felt like it. They almost had everything ready.

He took plenty of time before he called his driver. When he arrived, it was about ten. He told him that he wanted to go to the lawyer's office again and he could wait for him. There was a coffee shop in the building. He could go there. He would come there when he was ready to go.

When he got there, the lady told him to go on in. He tapped on the door and went in. The lawyer asked him about a few things he wanted to straighten out, then Joe took time to look over the papers, making sure everything was in order. He would never sign anything unless he was sure it was in the right order. Then he signed everything and passed them back to the lawyer.

He told the lawyer that next month he was going back to Newfoundland for a month if his health held out okay, and they could keep everything running smoothly. They should take out their fee for the work they did and it seemed like there was a load off his shoulders. He was happy about what he'd done. He'd had a good life and enjoyed it, but now Myrtle was gone and not much seemed to matter. He would go back with Bill and enjoy a good holiday where no one knew anything about him, because he never expected to make another trip.

Chapter 9

Bill grew up in the house where he lived. It was his father and mother's home. His father got lost on a schooner when Bill was in his early teens and his mother had to go to work to help raise him. But his mother said that his grandfather would send her money quite often to help her out, or so she told him.

Bill went to school and got all the grades he could get. Then he went to work with the town.

Sadie grew up next door. They were always friends. When they were six or seven, they took each other's hand and walked to school. After they grew up, they still hung around together and after Bill turned twenty, Bill said to Sadie, "We have always been together and I don't want to be with anyone else. Sadie, I love you. Would you marry me?"

She said, "I would jump at the chance, Bill. I've always loved you and couldn't do anything without you. Let's set a date so we can tell your mother and my father and brother." Her mother had passed on a few years back.

"Would next month be too soon?" Bill said.

"Not with me" she said. "Bill, do we want a large wedding? I would just like a small wedding with just a few friends."

"Just what I'd like," Bill said. "Bruce can be our best man. Jessie can be your bridesmaid if it is okay with you?"

"That would be just fine."

After the wedding, Sadie moved in with Bill as his mother was sick quite a lot of the time and that would make it better for Bill and his mother. Although Sadie and Bill were working, they could manage things between them and his mother did some work at home when she could.

Things worked out fine for them both, but now Sadie's father was on his own with his son who was still home and had never married. They were both cooks and could do well without Sadie.

After a few months, Bill's mother grew sicker than ever, ending up in the hospital where the doctor said she had cancer and only gave her a few months to live. She called Bill in and told him what the doctor said, but right then, she felt very good. If the doctor approved it, she wanted to come home for a while. Bill said, "We will check with the doctor and if he thinks you can, that will be good."

Sadie said, "You will be okay at home. I will see to that. And maybe you will get to church sometimes when you feel up to it."

"That will be wonderful," Annie said.

So after the doctor approved it, she got dressed and they left for home. Annie said, "I have a little business to see to after we get home." Bill did not know what she meant. She was feeling fairly good.

As soon as they got home, Annie went to her room and came out with papers. She said to Bill, "Here Bill. As soon as you can get a day off, take these papers in to the lawyer and get them changed over to your name. I will sign them for you before something happens to me."

Bill still had days coming to him from working overtime at the council, so he took them off and went into town. Sadie stayed with Mother. Bill got everything changed over to his name as his mother had told him to do. The lawyer told him to get a JP or a minister to be there when she signed the deed to make it legal.

Bill was feeling bad that his mother knew her time was short because she was so sick. The doctor only gave her a short time to live, but she took it all well and wanted to have everything fixed up for Bill before it was too late. She said that was her main worry. She had nothing to live for now that her husband was gone and she was ready to go. She had always been a Christian. The minister came to visit her and while he was there, they signed all the papers. Everything worked out just fine. They never had to go and find a JP to sign with them.

It was good they did it then, because that night they had to rush her back to the hospital. Bill and Sadie stayed with her for a couple of days. Jessie told them to stay at her home, which was only ten minutes from the hospital. Two day later, when they weren't with her at the hospital, she was gone.

Chapter 10

Bill and Sadie left the hospital and went back to Jessie's. Now his mother was gone. He had to contact his grandfather and Jessie had his phone number. Bill had never talked with him, but Jessie had, so he would ask Jessie to phone him.

When they got to Jessie's, she said, "Bill, your mother is gone. I can see it in your eyes."

"Yes," Bill said, "she is gone and we will surely miss her."

Jessie looked up the phone number for his grandfather and gave him a ring, but there was no answer.

"We will have a lunch, then I will try again," and she did, but never got any answer that day. The next day Bill had to go and prepare for the funeral, so he left in the morning for home. He told Jessie to keep trying. She never got hold of him until the day of the funeral.

He told her how badly he felt and there was no way

he could make it down now. He told Jessie to tell Bill that he was sending down enough money to cover the cost of the funeral and would talk to Bill later.

Making a call to Bill, Jessie told him what his grandfather had said. Bill was glad that she got in touch with him. It seemed like he was a busy man and hard to contact, but he understood him not coming down, as it would take almost a week to get there.

Jessie came out to the funeral and stayed all night with Bill and Sadie. There were a lot of people who visited them that evening and the next day, and Jessie could help with giving them coffee and sandwiches.

After a week, Bill went back to work and things began to get back to normal. Sadie went back to the things she was involved in around town. Although she wasn't feeling that well herself, she couldn't tell Bill how she felt. He already had enough trouble and she didn't want to put any more on him. He first lost his cousin in an auto crash, then his father went missing on the boat, and now his mother was gone. Plus he was trying to work all hours on heavy equipment with the town. She was hoping she never had serious trouble and guessed she was nervous now, but she was still a young woman.

Now Grandfather was there for a month. He said he might never get back again on a trip as he was getting too old to travel and he could see that Sadie was not feeling well, although she told him they really would like him to stay longer, maybe another month. Joe never told them, but he had things to look after back in the States. He sure enjoyed his time there and how well they treated him.

Chapter 11

Bill and Sadie made a few trips to New York after Grandfather passed on to see to the business affairs that were left to Bill. Jessie also came along as Grandfather told the lawyer, but she left everything up to Bill.

Bill went alone this time because Sadie was feeling sick and she thought it was best for him to go alone. Her father was next door with her brother and if she wanted anything, they were there. Jessie said she would come and spend some time with Sadie as well.

So Bill went on to New York. He had to spend two weeks there. He stayed at one of his hotels, as there were five. When he went to see the lawyer, the lawyer told him he had good or bad news for him. There was a company building high-rises and wanted to buy the hotels. In fact, they were willing to buy Bill's firm if he would sell, because they were expanding fast and could use the sites. They were planning on building on one of the sites where one of Bill's hotels sat and if he would sell, they would leave the others as they were making money. However, they might add more rooms.

They had come in and asked if they could appraise what the firm owned. They were willing to pay two hundred and twenty-two million for everything and take over the firm, but the lawyer would like to buy the building that housed his offices.

"Well," Bill said, "if you want this building, do all the paperwork to sell the firm and everything I have, including grandfather's home. Now Sam has passed away, let that go as well. Make out separate papers for this place paying one hundred dollars to make it legal.

"I am staying for a while, so you can talk to them and tell them what I want to do. When you do talk to them and if they want to go through with it, I will stay until it is all sold."

A week later Bill received a phone call from the lawyer requesting that he come to the office. He had everything sold and was ready for Bill to sign the papers and receive the money to deposit in his bank. As soon as Bill arrived at the office, the lawyer was ready and was happy that Bill made him the deal for the building, because now it was their own. They would collect the rent and the buyers were happy with the deal as well.

After Bill had everything signed, he went to the bank and had most of the money transferred to his bank back in Newfoundland. Then he checked out of his hotel and asked his driver to take him to the airport to catch his flight back home.

After landing at the airport, he picked up his car and baggage and drove home. He was glad to be back and to have a rest with nothing to worry about back in the United States. He would rather be out in his strawberry patch.

Jessie had gone home and Sadie was feeling fair and after a good night's sleep and rest, they both went into town to check on the bank. On the way in they picked up Jessie because Bill wanted to give her what belonged to her.

After picking up Jessie, they went on to the bank and checked out his account. Sure enough the money was there. He transferred quite a large sum to Jessie and she was really pleased as his grandfather never had to leave her anything.

Then they went to a good restaurant, had a lovely meal and left for home, dropping Jessie off on the way and asking her to come out tomorrow and spend a few days with them.

Chapter 12

Bill still had a few days of holidays coming to him, so before they were all over he went to the council and told them he was quitting his job with them as his grandfather had left him a good pension and he could live on that. Someone may have needed the job more than he did.

They told him they were sorry to see him go, but they were glad for him.

Bill was glad to stay off, because Sadie was feeling miserable most of the time and if he was home he could help her with some of the things she thought she had to do. She wanted Jessie there as long as she would stay. She loved Jessie and often wished she would move in with them, because she treated her so good now that she was sick.

Jessie was involved in many things where she lived and unless she forgot about them, she could only come once a month. But when she could, she did come to help Sadie, her best friend.

Sadie's brother was now caretaker of the place when Bill went away anywhere. Bill made sure they were paid to help him out. He lived next door and if Bill were working out in the garden where he loved to be, her brother would come over to talk and help if Bill wanted him. Now Bill had less worries, so he spent a lot of his time working in the workshop and garden, enjoying life and the things he never had the time to do before.

This morning Sadie's brother came over to help in the garden while Sadie said she would cook a meal for them. Now she had help as Bill hired a girl because of Sadie's sickness, but Sadie wanted to help today and have her father and brother in to the meal with them. Bill thought it was a great idea. He told Sadie, "Let the girl do the work, just tell her what to do." But Sadie felt fairly good and helped, and when the meal was ready, she went over to her father's and told him to come over for dinner. Then she went to the garden to get her brother and Bill, and on the way back she fell down. They thought she only tripped in the rough ground and fell, but when they tried to pick her up, she was gone. Bill told her brother to ring for an ambulance as fast as he could while he worked on her trying to bring her back.

In a short while the ambulance was there and the drivers worked on her. Then they took her on board and went right to the hospital. The doctor checked her out and said she'd had a massive heart attack. Bill followed the ambulance in. The doctor said, "Bill, I am sorry. Your wife is gone." Bill was devastated to the point he was in shock. One of the drivers had to drive his car back home for him. When he got home, her father and brother were waiting. It was hard to believe. She never thought that her heart was bad and she would not go for a checkup. Someone phoned Jessie and Jessie almost fainted with the news. It was hard for her to believe knowing she was sick, but not thinking that was the trouble. Bill said she had gone home to be with the Lord. That is what she lived for. Sadie was a good Christian.

Now Sadie's father and brother helped to get the funeral arrangements ready. Bill almost had a heart attack himself. The doctor had to give him medication to keep him going. Everyone belonging to him was gone, and now Sadie. He was alone in the world. He and Sadie were so happy together. But that was life. Just when they got ready to live, she was gone.

He went to school hand-in-hand with her when they were kids. They grew up together. His schoolgirl sweetheart was gone. It was hard to hold himself together, but for the sake of her brother and father, he had to try to do his best.

Two weeks after the funeral he was sitting alone in the home where he had spent most of the past two weeks just trying to get things back on track. He had told the girl who always came in to help do the work with Sadie that he did not need her now. She could pick up her paycheck at Sadie's father's house, because he would be away.

He then went to the funeral home to pay up the funeral expenses and any other bill that needed to be paid. He would have to try and start living without Sadie, which was the hardest thing he ever had to do. Then he came back home. He hardly knew what to do next. He then rang Jessie, not to start a relationship with her, but just for someone to talk to. She answered the phone with the words, "Bill, I have been thinking about you and wondering how you were making out. I have almost been sick to my stomach with the shock of Sadie's passing. I will surely miss her and miss visiting her. I loved her. She was my best friend."

Bill felt a little better after talking to Jessie. She encouraged him to try and pick up the pieces. He still had to carry on. That is what Sadie would want him to do. Then Bill went over to Sadie's father and brother's to see how they were feeling. They were fair, telling Bill to pull himself together. Her father told him that he had lost Sadie's mother, but had to make out the best he could. He told him, "You still have us here whenever you want something. We will look after everything if you go away and you still have Jessie to talk to. She is one of the finest women around." Bill knew that she was more like a sister to him than a friend.

Chapter 13

Bill was still living alone. Sadie's brother now had married the girl who was working for Bill and was living at her father's house. As he had him as caretaker, his wife came and did the work around the house for him and looked after the place so Bill never had to worry about anything there.

Now Bill would go into town and sometimes spend a week there. As he never had to worry about money, he would stay at a hotel, but did visit Jessie when there. He never had anyone over to visit.

He did some investing in the stock market and other things, which took him into town maybe once every month. He also wanted to see how Jessie was making out.

It had been almost two years now since Sadie passed on. He was trying to carry on. He loved her very much and did everything to make her happy, but as her father told him, he would have to carry on and live, maybe get another woman. He couldn't live alone forever. He knew all this and it was a lonely life.

He liked Jessie a lot and he knew that Jessie liked him. They were never close enough to have an affair. Bill was a Christian and wanted to live right and follow in his mother's footsteps. Jessie was also a Christian, but he spent a lot of time with her and now she would come home with him and spend time there. She also visited Sadie's father and brother.

Sadie's father said, "Jessie, you should marry Bill now."

She blushed and said, "What would you think if I did that?"

He said, "I think it would be the best thing he could do."

"We will see down the road what will happen. After all, I was his cousin's wife."

He said, "There is no blood relationship there.

"What are we talking about? Bill never talked about marrying."

After going back to Bill's, they had dinner together that Sadie's brother had cooked for them. He stayed to eat with them too.

While at dinner, Bill said, "You are here today for something special. That is the reason I asked you. Today is our big day."

After sitting down and blessing the food, Bill said, "Before we eat, I want to do something." He put his hand in his pocket and took out a small package. He opened it up and took out a ring set and said, "Jessie, this is an engagement ring. Will you marry me?"

Jessie eyes filled with tears. She was so excited. "Yes, Bill. I have been waiting for you to ask."

"Well, this is the wedding ring you will get when we do marry. I will leave it up to you as to the time."

She said as soon as they could get things ready.

"Bill, I would rather not have a big thing, just a small affair if that would be okay with you?"

"Just what I want," Bill said. So they ate their dinner and celebrated their engagement with Bill's brother-in-law. Then Bill asked them if they would stand up for them when they got married.

Jim said, "Sure will. Just let me know when."

Bill got things ready with Jessie for the wedding. She had to go into town to get a new dress and go to her home and get a few things.

After seeing a minister, Bill and Jessie planned the wedding in three days. Then they were going to New York to spend a few days and see a few friends they had made while there, and Bill still had business to do at the bank.

It was only a quiet wedding with just a few people there, and it was just what they both wanted with about twelve guests. Some of the fellows and their wives from the council where Bill worked came and his father-in-law looked so happy that he said what he did.

After it was all over, they got Jim to drive them in to catch a flight to New York.

Chapter 14

Landing in New York they got a cab to take them to the hotel that he once owned. Now they booked in as man and wife, whereas before they had separate rooms. It was their honeymoon.

They had a lovely dinner and a lovely evening together, then retired for the night. Jessie and Bill both said they were acting like teenagers, but it was a great day for both of them and they had to forget the past and carry on.

The next day Bill hired a driver to take him around who knew the city better than him. Bill told him to take him to the bank, giving him the address. They both went into the bank and saw the manager. They asked him to transfer more money back to the Newfoundland Bank, which he did. Right then Bill wasn't spending all the interest he was getting, so they lived it up for a few days.

They went and saw the lawyer at his office and had

to wait for twenty minutes. Bill just had to see him and hear all the news about the people who bought him out. They both went into the lawyer's office, telling the lawyer this was Jessie and now that his first wife had passed away, he had married her.

After asking the lawyer about everything, the lawyer said, "The people who bought you out have extended on some of the hotels and demolished the other one to build the high-rise. They are in the money.

There are still opportunities here if you wish to invest. Bill thanked him and said they were going back to Newfoundland to take life a little easier and enjoy things back there. "We don't want to get into anything else now, only travel around when we feel like it."

Then they shook hands and Bill and Jessie went to the best hotel around and had dinner, telling the driver to come back in an hour and a half to pick them up.

After spending a week going around shopping and so on, they thought it was time for them to go back home.

They phoned the airport and they said there was a flight out in the morning if they were ready to pay first class. "That will be good," Bill said. "Book us in for two people." They told him to be there at seven-thirty. "Fine," Bill said, telling the person at the desk to make sure to call them tomorrow morning around six o'clock and that he wanted breakfast then because he had to catch a flight out at seven-thirty.

They went to bed early. It seemed like they'd just gotten in bed when the phone rang for them to get up. After a shower they were ready for breakfast. Then the driver that he had hired took them to the airport. By the time they got there, they just had time to get the tickets and pay the driver, and rush onboard the plane.

Bill said, "I had a fine trip. I don't know about

you?"

Jessie said it was good, but a little tiring. "I enjoyed it," Jessie said, "but the trouble is we are both getting older and we just can't take it like we used to."

"When we get back, we can take things easier and relax," Bill said.

Landing back at the airport, Jim was waiting for them. Bill had phoned him and told him when they would get there. They both felt relaxed now to be back where they had lived most of their lives. They had to pass by Jessie's home, so Jessie said she would like to check on the place if she could. "Sure," Bill said, "and have a cup of tea if you wish." He asked Jim if there was plenty of time or did he have anything to do he had to get back for.

Jim said, "If you say stay, I stay. If you say go, I go. You pay me well and I am at your service."

"Well," Bill said, "Come on in. We'll use up some of Jessie's food she has stored away."

Jessie said, "I haven't brought in very much lately as I have been spending so much time with you, but I think we can find enough for a cup of tea and a few crackers."

By the time they got home to Bill's, it was well after dark and the house was lit right up. Jim's wife, Serah, had cooked a big meal for them. They told Jim to get his father and come over and enjoy the meal with them. Then after Serah cleaned up all the mess, they all left. Jessie and Bill were all alone. They spent the evening just relaxing and watching TV.

Chapter 15

Jessie asked Bill what was the best thing to do with her home in St. John's. Bill asked her about the people next door. They watched it whenever she was away. Bill said, "Maybe we could keep it for when we go into town. It would be somewhere to stay. We may want to spend more time in there by keeping the house. I will never spend the money I have, but I don't want to throw it away. We can pay those people to keep watching it for us."

So they kept the house and sometimes they would spend two or three weeks in there. Between the two places they were enjoying life to the fullest.

Bill still had money invested and by being in St. John's he could see to things better. When they were tired of town they would come back to Bill's home and they both would spend time working in the garden.

They talked about what would happen when they were gone. They would have to get wills made out to someone and get a lawyer to be the administrator of the estates. Bill asked her if she had any relations around that she would want to leave it to. Jessie said that she had one, a nephew, who was a fine fellow and that was it. Bill said, "The only ones I have are Jim and his father. We could have it split between your nephew and Jim. If something happens to us both at the same time, or whatever does happen, they will get it. We will go into town tomorrow and get things fixed up.

They left the first thing in the morning and made an appointment to see the lawyer for that day at two o'clock. When they got there he was waiting for them. They told him what they wanted, giving him all the details. He told them to give him a day and he would have it ready.

So Bill and Jessie went back to her home for the night, but they went to a restaurant first and had a meal as they never had much food at the house. It was better to go out and buy meals for a couple of days, but they did enjoy cooking their own meals together.

The next afternoon they checked with the lawyer. He had everything ready for them to sign. After signing everything they took their copies and went to the bank and put them in a safety deposit box.

They went back home that evening without any worries. In the next few months they became involved in whatever volunteer work they could find around town and church, and were very happy. After all the things that had happened in their lives, there were times when it was awfully rough, but now they thanked the Lord that everything worked out and they were happy together and were both Christians.

Chapter 16

Jake owned a hotel just on the edge of the town where Bill and Jessie lived. Many times Bill and Jessie would go there for dinner. The food was good and as Jake had worked with Bill, they were friends. They would often chat about the things they worked at. Both were heavy equipment operators and had things in common.

On this day when Bill and Jessie came for dinner, Jake asked them if they would care if he sat with them and had his dinner. They would love it, they both said. In the conversation, Jake said he was planning on selling out, as he had other interests and he was not a hotel man. He was only just holding his own and not making any money. Bill said he would miss him. It was too bad he had to sell. That's all that was said about it. They ate their dinner and went home.

Jessie said, "Bill, there must be something wrong as to why they can't money. They seem to have lots of people coming and going there…"

Bill never gave her time to finish before he said, "Maybe we should buy it."

Both Jessie and Bill knew that they would have to do something. They always worked and there was a big void now with nothing to do, only run around and do the gardens. Although they loved to work in the garden, there was not enough volunteer work to keep them busy.

"Guess this is our chance to get something to work at," Bill said. "I will give Jake a call and make an appointment with him, and we can talk it over about the price. By the way he sounds, it will be a good buy." Bill had some of his grandfather's way about him. He just had to make money and thought if he had the place he could make it pay.

Bill gave Jake a call and asked him if he was still selling the hotel. Jake said, "Yes, if I can get a buyer." Bill asked what time could Jessie and he come and talk to him about it. Jake said, "Tomorrow afternoon. I will be here. I am leaving for St. John's this evening, but will be back by noon tomorrow."

Bill said, "That will be fine." Jake told Bill he could come there this evening and one of the staff would show him around the place so he would have a good idea what the place was like. "Good," said Bill, "I will do that."

Around four Jessie and Bill went to the hotel to have dinner and look around. One of the staff took them around. The lady was very courteous and Bill thought if they were all like that, they were a good staff.

The hotel had twenty-two rooms and at the present time about half were full, which looked good for that time of the year, because it was the slack time.

Going back to the dining room and having dinner, they talked about it. If Jake didn't have his price too high, they would buy. They really enjoyed the meals there. The cooks were good and the staff looked like the best. Jake had them well trained.

They went back home and relaxed watching TV for a while until someone from the church rang Jessie and asked her and Bill if they would come and help. They were getting ready for a marriage and needed someone to help to decorate the church. It was just what they needed to help pass the night and get out with friends. It was close to midnight when they were through and it was off to bed to sleep on everything that was happening.

Although they were now used to doing business, it was a little exciting and they both woke up quite early. They got out of bed and had a shower and breakfast. Bill still loved to work in his workshop, so he spent a couple of hours there while Jessie was poking around the house.

He thought he heard Jessie call and he opened the door and looked out. Jessie said, "You know what time it is?" He was so taken up with what he was doing that he forgot the time. It was twelve. He closed the door and went to the house. He gave Jake a call and told him that he was sorry, but he would be a little late for the appointment. He told him what he did. Jake told him that he would be there all evening and anytime was okay with him.

They took plenty of time now that he had phoned Jake to change and get ready for lunch. Jake was at the front desk when they went into the hotel. Jake said to go and have their lunch, because he had plenty of time that evening.

They had a real good lunch and met a person that

they knew from St. John's and enjoyed their company. The person was staying there at the hotel while doing business in town.

When the lunch was finished, they went to the office where Jake was. "Come in," Jake said, "and make yourselves comfortable," which they did. Jake asked them if they went through the hotel and how everything looked to them. Jake told them that most everything was in good repair, but might need some work. Bill said it looked fair from what he saw. Jake kept talking about everything but the price.

Finally he came to the price. He told Bill the hotel was valued at three hundred thousand, but he was selling for two hundred thousand with five acres of land.

"Well," Bill said, "what do you think, Jessie?"

"Bill, you know more about it than I do."

"I think we will go through with it and buy. As soon as you get the papers ready, we are ready."

Jake said, "I will make the trip to St. John's tomorrow and have the papers made ready. As soon as they are done I will give you a call. I will advise the staff that you are buying. You can come in tomorrow and get in on the running of the place if you care to, so when you take over you will know what to do or expect."

"Fine," Bill said, "we will do that."

The next morning they were in quite early and had breakfast there at the hotel. Then they went to work getting to know all the staff and checking out what each one did, who worked at this and who worked at that.

By the end of the day, Bill had most everything under control and was ready for the next move, which was signing the papers.

Chapter 17

Going to St. John's to see his lawyer and also Jake's lawyer, and paying and signing all the papers, made him the owner of a hotel again. It was not so large as the hotels in New York, but a good start here at home.

They went to Jessie's home and stayed there all night planning their next move. Jessie was an accountant, working at an accountant's office when she was younger. For now she would work at the office. He would look after things around the hotel, but as soon as he could get a good hotel manager, he would hire him so he could have free time to move on. He and Jessie had decided that they were going to add on more hotels whenever the price was right.

The hotel had a large convention room that had to be kept busy. They had to do a lot of advertising to put the hotel on the map. If his grandfather could make money, so could he, and he had to. His grandfather maybe had meant for him to carry on with the business and he would, but not in New York. It would be better here at home in Newfoundland, which was the place where he wanted to live.

After a month he had a good hotel manager hired and he was doing a good job. Everything was running smoothly and the staff got along with him well. Their morale was up and with the advertising he did, the place was beginning to make money.

He never wanted to see the hotel fail. It employed quite a few people from the town where he lived and he wanted to keep them employed. That was his main goal.

Now Jessie didn't have to keep the accounting job at the hotel. He arranged with his law firm to look after that so he could find other projects.

They were two good business people. They both had business minds. They already had other investments in the town of St. John's, like an apartment building with forty-eight apartments. They had a live-in manager there and everything was running smoothly.

He thought now it was time that he should get his business incorporated and that was the next step. He needed to go into St. John's to see his lawyer and get the job done. He would take a salary to oversee it all.

He and Jessie went to St. John's the very next day, saw the lawyer and had the papers drawn up to form the company with Jim having a share and also Jessie's nephew. Bill would have a salary of one hundred and twenty thousand a year and Jessie would always be by his side helping with whatever she could. She would get a salary as well and Jim was already getting paid for being the caretaker of Bill's own home and was quite happy. Her nephew was just a shareholder and would get his share at the end of the year if the company made any money.

Jessie and Bill had a little more time for themselves now. They could travel around and watch out for more things to add to their list.

His grandfather had a keen mind and had built up quite an empire in New York. He would do the same thing here. It was not that there was anything wrong with New York, the people were good and they treated him well, but it was Newfoundland for him.

He kept buying hotels and employing people until he had about twelve hotels and a construction company with a million dollars' worth of heavy equipment and a large sawmill. It was all paid for from his earnings.

Now he still had the money his grandfather left him. He only used it to buy and put it back when the company made money.

Chapter 18

Grandfather was either smart or he was at the right place at the right time, because he sure made money. After leaving it all to Jessie and Bill, they put it to good use and also made money. Bill's company was worth many millions now and Bill was getting paid two hundred and seventy thousand a year. Jessie was getting one hundred thousand.

Bill asked Jim if he would like to do what he was doing by looking after the affairs of the company. Jim said he would rather stay where he was. He couldn't handle it.

Bill was now getting older and within the last fifteen years he had built up a large company and would love to have a good man to carry on and do what he was doing so he could sit back and just watch things. Both he and Jessie would like to just take it easy.

Bill asked Jessie about her nephew. Although he was a shareholder, he only knew very little about him.

Jessie said he had been working with the same company for years. Maybe they should call him and have him come for an interview. Maybe he was just the man to take over.

Bill called Fred that evening, asking him if he would make a trip out, he would like to see him. Fred agreed to come out on the weekend

On Saturday Fred did come. He knew all about Bill and the large company he had built up because of the money he received every year from being a shareholder.

Bill asked Fred all about himself and what he was doing, and about the company he worked for. After all the questions, Bill said, "Fred, how would you like a job like I have, going around just making sure things are running smoothly?"

Fred said, "I guess it would be a good job. There'd be plenty of worries I guess, but that's what one gets paid for."

"Well," Bill said, "would you take over my job if you were asked?"

"I would give it a try. I am owed a month of holidays. I could try it out for that month."

"Okay, as soon as you are ready, you can come in and make your rounds with me to learn all about our company. If you like it and prove out, you will get two hundred and fifty thousand dollars a year plus the interest on your shares at the end of the year. So, the more money the company makes, the more you make. It will be just up to you to make sure the company is making money."

Fred said, "It is a big challenge, but I believe I can do it. I will do my best. I know I could never fill your shoes, because you have some of your wealthy grandfather's spirit, but I will sure try."

Fred came the following week and sat with Bill as he went around to all of his company's sites checking on some of the hotels that he owned and checking the construction sites. They went all around the island.

It took about a week to cover it all. Once they got home, Fred went back to his home. Bill told Fred to come back again on Monday and he would pass the car over to him. Bill would ride along with him as Fred checked things out and he would stay in the background while Fred talked to all the managers. Fred had now met them all and they knew that he was the new man in charge. After that, Fred could do it alone.

Fred felt sort of out of place, but he had to take himself by the collar and forget Bill was there. He needed to do what he thought was right and so far as Bill was concerned, he did well.

Bill told Fred, "It is all in your hands now. Your salary started the first day you started. Your check will come in the mail from the lawyer's office. You don't have to check with me anymore now unless there is something you may want advice on. I will be always be here to help if you need me.

"I may make a trip around once in a while, but I will not interfere with you in any way. It will just be a pleasure trip for Jessie and I. It is hard to get it out of my bones, so don't worry if you see me sometimes. You are in charge and I know you can do it and make money, and if you see us at any time in your rounds, we are not checking on you, we are just enjoying running around."

Bill knew from the start he now had a good man at the wheel. He shook Fred's hand as he left knowing now that he and Jessie would relax a little more and enjoy just doing what they liked. They kept up with what his grandfather had done. They built up a good company and gave quite a lot of people a good living. That was the best of it. He could go to church and sit with any one of his employees with a clear conscious, because he paid them well and also made money.

Bill was having dinner at the hotel with Jessie one day and enjoying it. He said, "Jessie, my wealthy grandfather, Joe, never saw all this when he went to New York to look for work as a carpenter. But, when opportunities came along he made good on it and became very wealthy. I believe he would be happy to know that I have carried on and done my best to follow in his shoes. Jessie, I believe that Fred will do the same. He is young and he will come up with new ideas where now my mind is getting stale. It is now time to get out and enjoy some of the money we have before it is too late. It is all up to the fellows I have put in charge now to make a living for themselves. We have all we will ever want and we are still in love and going to church whenever we can. We're enjoying life here in a small town where everyone knows everyone and are happy that we decided to stay here. Grandfather did say the last time he was home here to Newfoundland that old soldiers never die, they just fade away. And if you are happy, I am happy.

Bill's company did get stronger and grew while Bill and Jessie got older. Then they did just that, they faded out of the picture and everyone came to Fred for everything.

CPSIA information can be obtained
at www.ICGtesting.com
Printed in the USA
LVHW010519251019
635283LV00001B/12/P